ANT SCHOOL

JOEY'S SCHOOL

STORM DRAIN

INSIDE ANDY'S HOME

SIDE WALK

HALLWAY

LIGHT MITE

DINING ROOM

Dear
Did you ever borrow something
from somebody and not tell
them that you borrowed it?
That's what I did once and
I almost got in big trouble.
I Learned an important
Lesson and I'LL tell you
all about it.

Sincerely,
Joey

THE ADVENTURES OF Andy Ant™
The Band Music Mystery

Created by Lawrence W. O'Nan
Written by Gerald D. O'Nan
Illustrated by Norman McGary

Dedicated to Michelle Tiffany O'Nan

Tyndale House Publishers, Inc.
Wheaton, Illinois

First printing, August 1988. ISBN 0-8423-0315-4. Text and illustrations © 1988 by Andy Ant Productions. Andy Ant is a trademark of Andy Ant Productions, Inc. All rights reserved. Printed by Zrinski, Yugoslavia.

THE school band practice started at four o'clock and I was going to be late if I didn't hurry. I'd left my trumpet at home, so I had to ride my bike there as fast as I could to get it. Mr. Beck, the band teacher, always gets pretty mad if anyone is late. I know, 'cause I've been late before.

Just as I was getting back on my bike with my trumpet, I heard a small voice say, "Boy, am I ever glad to see you. I forgot my horn this morning. I won't make it to band practice on time unless you give me a lift on your bicycle." I looked down and there stood Andy Ant, with his tuba around his shoulders.

You see, Andy plays in the Grand Ant school band. He even practices every Wednesday after school, just like I do. So he needed to get there right away, too. Andy climbed onto my bicycle handlebars, and we headed back to the school.

On the way, Andy blew his horn every time a dog or cat got in our way. I was amazed that such a small tuba had such a big sound! It reminded me of a foghorn on a ship. Andy thought the sound was so neat that he started blowing his horn even when there weren't any dogs or cats around.

We made it back to school just in time and I sure was glad. I don't like to get yelled at. Andy started to run across the playground toward his school, then I heard him holler, "Angelica, you'd better hurry."

Angelica is Andy's older sister. She's in the sixth grade and she plays the flute in the Grand Ant band. At least, that's what she does some of the time. Andy says she spends most of the time talking to her friends. Maybe that's just the way sixth-grade ants act.

I walked into the band room and got my trumpet out of its case. Then I realized something terrible. I'd left my music at home! I couldn't believe it. The only thing that makes Mr. Beck madder than when you're late is when you don't have your music.

Then I remembered—Kenny Anderson's mom had taken him to the eye doctor to get glasses, so he wouldn't be at band practice today. I could use his music. He never practices at home, so I was

pretty sure it was at school. Sure enough, it was there, right where Kenny usually keeps his trumpet. "I can just borrow it," I said. "Nobody even needs to know. And this way I won't get in trouble for leaving mine at home!"

After that, everything seemed to go fantastic. I didn't even make mistakes during band practice. Then Mr. Beck made an announcement.

"We are going to do something special on Friday—we're going to have tryouts for concert band. So take your music home and practice!"

Wow! Concert band is for the kids who are really good, and I sure wanted to be in it. Then Mr. Beck said we could go, so I threw the music into my trumpet case and ran out the door. Andy was already sitting on my bicycle's handlebars and his tuba was over his shoulder. I guess he thought I wasn't hurrying enough so he gave me a couple of blasts on his horn.

"Can't you move any faster, Joey?" he asked. "I'm hungry and I want to get home before Angelica and her friends eat everything."

"Well, you could have walked home," I told him. "You didn't have to wait for me."

"Yeah, but I have to carry this big tuba and all Angelica has to carry is her flute." Andy looked up at me, trying to get some sympathy. I just smiled at him and hopped on my bike.

I pedaled home as fast as I could, but as we rode up the sidewalk we could see Angelica and her friends walking into Andy's house.

"There goes my snack," Andy said, disgusted. "Angelica always takes my Vita Crumbs and gives them to her friends. She says she's just 'borrowing' them, but I never see them again."

"Why don't you come over to my house?" I said. "I'm sure we can find plenty to eat."

Andy seemed to think that was a good idea. He ran inside to put his tuba away, then jumped on my right sneaker and we went inside.

Mom was in the kitchen, so I grabbed some milk and cookies and headed for my room. I figured Andy would feel more comfortable there.

"Don't get any crumbs on the floor," Mom said as I was leaving. "You know that always brings those messy ants inside."

Andy looked like he was going to say something to my mom, but I frowned at him and shook my head. "I'll be careful, Mom," I told her and turned to leave.

"Don't forget to practice your trumpet before supper," she said as I headed for my room.

"I won't forget, Mom," I answered. "I'm going to practice a lot 'cause tryouts for concert band are on Friday."

I went into my room, closed the door, and took the milk and cookies over to my bed. In no time at all, Andy was sitting on top of the bedpost, eating his share.

"Boy, these cookies are terrific, Joey," Andy said as he stuffed another crumb into his mouth. "May I come over here every day after school?"

"Sure," I said, "just don't let my mom catch you. You know what she does to ants." Andy's mouth was so full of cookies that he couldn't say anything, so he just nodded his head.

I finished another cookie, then decided to practice my trumpet. I opened my case and guess what I found? Yep, Kenny Anderson's music—I'd forgotten to put it back. But I wasn't too worried, he probably wouldn't need it until next week anyway.

"Hey, Joey," Andy said as he swallowed the last of his cookies, "doesn't that music folder have Kenny Anderson's name on it?"

"Well . . . yeah. It's Kenny's music, I just borrowed it."

Andy frowned. "I didn't think Kenny liked you well enough to lend you a burned-out light bulb. Why would he lend you his music?"

"Well, uh, Kenny doesn't really know I borrowed it," I said.

"He doesn't know you have it?" Andy blurted out, jumping down from the bedpost. "He'll probably break your neck if he catches you with his music! Why did you take it?"

I started to explain what had happened, but just then my mom knocked and came into my room. Andy hid real fast—like I said, he knows what my mom does to ants.

"Joseph," Mom said. "Would you mind practicing your trumpet a little later? Kenny Anderson's mom is at the front door and she would like to borrow your music for a little while."

"Gee whiz, Mom," I said, "Kenny never practices at home. What does she want it for?"

"Mr. Beck called her to tell her about the tryouts and she wants Kenny to practice. She couldn't find Kenny's music at school, so she stopped by here since they live close to us."

"Well, couldn't I just take the music over later?" I asked, trying to push Kenny's music folder out of sight.

"Joseph, she's waiting at the front door. Please just give me the music!" And before I could stop her, Mom reached out and took the music folder and marched back to the front door.

"Oh no, what am I going to do now?" I said. "What if they think I stole Kenny's music?" I looked around for Andy. Since he is kind of a philosopher, he always seems to know the right thing to do. Maybe he would have some good advice for the mess I was in. But there was no sign of him, so I figured he must have gone home.

"Just my luck!" I said. "Whenever I want that ant around, he's not here. But if I didn't want him here, you can bet he'd show up, handing out his advice all over the place."

It wasn't that I didn't appreciate Andy's advice. I did—he was real smart for an ant, especially one who was only in the fourth grade. But I wanted to talk to him now! In fact, I guess I wanted him to be there so much that I thought I heard him call my name. But it was probably just my imagination, 'cause when I looked around I didn't see him anywhere.

I opened the door of my room a crack and listened. I could hear Mom talking with Mrs. Anderson at the front door. What was I going to do? One thing was for sure, the longer I waited the worse it was going to be. So I decided to go tell them what had happened. After all, that's probably what Andy would tell me to do.

When I walked into the front room, my mouth almost hit the floor. There, next to Mom and Mrs. Anderson, stood Kenny. As soon as he saw me he gave me one of those looks that let me know I was going to get it. They must have seen Kenny's name on the folder.

The only thing I could do was make sure they knew I'd only borrowed Kenny's music, not stolen it.

"Mom," I blurted out, "I didn't mean to take Kenny's music! It was an accident!" And I told them the whole story—how I forgot my music, then borrowed Kenny's, then forgot to put it back.

At first nobody said a word. They just stared at me like I'd turned green or something. Mom looked like she all of a sudden had an up-

set stomach. Mrs. Anderson didn't look much better. But Kenny looked just fine—like he wasn't even mad or anything.

"I'm real sorry I borrowed your music without asking," I told Kenny, hoping Andy was wrong about him wanting to break my neck.

"It's OK . . . this time," Kenny said.

Mom and Mrs. Anderson started smiling. "I'm glad you apologized, Joseph," Mom said. "We didn't notice Kenny's name on the folder. But I'm sure Kenny would have seen it once he got home."

"What?" I said, surprised. Then what were you talking about when I came in?"

Mrs. Anderson smiled. "We were talking about Kenny's new glasses. He's been worried that the other children would make fun of them." I looked at Kenny and he smiled. I hadn't even noticed his glasses, and I could tell he was glad.

After Kenny and his mom left, Mom turned to look at me.

"Well, Joseph, I think you've probably learned that it's not a good idea to borrow something without asking first."

"I sure have, Mom," I told her. "It feels crummy when you're afraid someone thinks you've stolen something. Next time, I'll take my chances with Mr. Beck."

Then I remembered I still needed to practice my trumpet for the tryouts. So I went back to my room, wishing Andy was around. I knew he'd be real proud of me for admitting what I'd done.

I picked up my trumpet and started practicing, but something was wrong. It sounded like something was stuck inside. So I blew real hard, and all of a sudden Andy flew out and landed on the music stand!

"Uh, hi, Joey," he said as he stood up and brushed himself off. "I suppose you were wondering what I was doing in your trumpet." I nodded and he continued. "Well, I jumped in it when your mom came to get Kenny's music and it was so dark in there that I got lost—and then I got stuck and couldn't get out. I tried calling you, but I guess you couldn't hear me."

"Well," I said, laughing, "it's a good thing you didn't jump into Kenny's music folder or you might have been stuck in there for a week until he opened it."

"So what are you going to do about that music?" Andy asked. "Have you figured out a way to keep Kenny from beating the tar out of you?"

"Oh, I think everything's going to be OK. Since you weren't around, I guessed what you would tell me to do and I did it."

"Well, let's hear what happened," Andy said as he climbed back up on the bedpost. He shoved his cap back and listened with great interest as I told him what had happened. I could tell he was really listening when I said I'd learned that it wasn't a good idea to borrow something without asking first.

"For a regular kid," Andy said, his face beaming approval, "you did all right. I just wish Angelica would learn the same lesson when it comes to my Vita Crumbs."

"If she asked you first, would you tell her she could have them?" I asked.

"Well, sure," Andy replied. "Then I could come to your house every day for snacks!"

We both laughed, and then I picked up my trumpet and started to practice again. Friday was coming fast, and I wanted to be ready for those tryouts.

Dad

Mom

Angelica

Uncle Andrew

Parker

Dickter

Your Friend,
Andy

Andy's Family (Me)